BETTY AND THE ANGELS OF THE HORIZON

BRYSON ARNOTT

© Bryson Arnott 2023

All rights reserved. No part of this publication may be reproduced, distributed, or transmitted in any form or by any means, including photocopying, recording, or other electronic or mechanical methods, without the prior written permission of the publisher, except in the case of brief quotations embodied in critical reviews and certain other noncommercial uses permitted by copyright law.

For Freya Konecny

TABLE OF CONTENTS

CHAPTER 1

NEW YEAR

On December 31 2007 Betty woke up early. It was nearly the new year and that day Betty had breakfast at the cafeteria. She had four lessons before her first twenty minute break, then six more lessons, lunch at the cafeteria, nine more lessons, another twenty minute break, three final lessons, then dinner at the cafeteria but instead of going to bed, that day she went outside to the mountain that Betty's school was on.

It was the New Year's Eve party. The school choir were learning to say happy New Years in 200 Languages. The people who were not afraid of heights were learning how to make fire rockets. The people who were afraid of heights were learning how to make campfires. There was a thing for everyone at that school.

Betty noticed that Ms A-lar was in the school spa and that Mr and Mrs Bark would love it if they were there. In order to guard the school so people could not escape, there were creepy statues that looked like the night jogger but even creepier. No-one, not even one person, would believe that Betty saw the night jogger. The night jogger was so famous around there because the funeral was hosted at that school and only four people went. Now it was getting late at the New Year's Eve party.

CHAPTER 2

THE HORIZON

The next day, Betty woke up just like when she found the secret room. A few seconds later a man knocked. "Betty I have something to show you". The person outside was the same person as last time!

Betty opened the door and followed Jace down the corridor to the lobby. It looked like they were going the same way as last time but they were getting sucked in, pulled down by two bars to another path before falling in a really sandy place.

It was very hot. "This Desert is mostly for the animals" Jace snorted. Betty laid down on a blanket they brought along. Betty watched the animals who were friendly, scary, dark and light plus that was only one habitat for all of the them.

Jace showed Betty the angel posters. They were like graveyard stones but in the desert. "I heard that the angels are flying a long way... I guess we will have to take down the angel posters..." sniffled Jace. "I'm sorry to hear that" said Betty. "Come on Betty, we will have to get back to your house now".

Before they left, Betty and Jace went to school street and got the guide book for the horizon. Soon Betty wondered if they were flying away from the school as it was only the next night when Betty was leaving.

CHAPTER 3

THE NEW YEARS LEAVE

Betty was taking her first walk back of her ninth year, down a horrible smelling road only a few people lived on. It was six miles away from the forest that the Barks lived by. There were nine people, hidden beneath the street in an underground hotel that Betty was standing on.

"Food?" quivered a voice from the underground hotel. They had a whole conversation and Betty gave him some food. Just then, a black spot appeared on the grey floor between two drains. Betty saw a strange light in between the two drains. Maybe it was a person coming to hurt her. Maybe even the night jogger.

A terrible pain rushed through Betty's head thinking of all the times the night jogger nearly hurt Betty. A nice breath of fresh air should have been good but that actually made it worse.

Betty ran to a nearby shop called '26 needs of all the lost worlds'. Inside were strange books that Betty could not read it because they were covered by muddy wet leaves. It was soon the time that Betty should be home or Mrs Bark would be worried. Betty's green hair started to spin and she teleported back to her home.

CHAPTER 4

BETTY'S FIRST SCHOOL TRIP

It was finally time for Betty's first school trip. Before going, they had quickly gone home to get their clothes. While there, they drank a drink that tasted different for everyone who tried it. Luckily for Betty, it tasted like a fresh piece of sweet cherry cake.

The coach ride there was super bumpy, in fact it was hard to stand up but when they sat down it felt like they were sitting on a blueberry pie. Most children fell asleep but Betty did not. They were on the coach for two hours and a half hours before they finally got off the coach and getting off was much harder then getting on.

Betty and the other children were going to a famous forest. It was famous because it was ancient and underground mines ran through it.

Betty reached a part of the forest that was hard to walk in. A temple that once stood there broke apart 200 years ago leaving lots of rubble. When they had finished walking on those ancient pieces of temple, Betty had a head-ache. The hard forest floor and the long coach ride had been a lot.

Past a large tree, they saw the part of the temple that was not destroyed. It had a tower which was once part of the temple and luckily they were able to climb to the top of it. Betty took a few deep breathes. She could see the whole forest from up here.

It was time to head back to the coach. They had forty minutes to get back to the car park and still had to get back past the the ancient temple pieces and through the forest. They made it back with only one minute to go and got on the coach. The ride home was much better.

CHAPTER 5

THE HORIZON'S ANGEL

Betty wanted to go back to the horizon because she didn't want to miss anything. Luckily Betty did not get caught getting there and now she was at the horizon. Betty decided to have a walk around. She was walking for over four miles before she saw a note crumpled on the floor. The note read...

'23 January 2008

To: Fla-mar Tiko/cleaning man

I would like to tell you about the local area, also known as the school horizon.

This is a very isolated area and I know that because all of the angels have dug themselves into the sand. Something bad might live in this area, and they are trying to hurt the angels.

Thank you, Mrs Mentle-fringe'

Betty felt a giant pain upon reading this note. She looked up and realised she was surrounded by spiders. Betty read in a book about the horizon that those spiders are called ETS and that baby ETS are less than a inch, child ETS are the size of a light switch and grown up ETS reach up to four feet tall. They looked like bad creatures when they were coming towards Betty.

Just then, an enormous white bird with two giant claws swooped down from above. It had a note hanging from its mouth that read 'I am the horizon angel'. The ETS had all scattered.

Betty was scared. The horizon angel was bad news and had lots of poisonous venom. She went to get her umbrella out and launch it at the angel, but it had mysteriously disappeared.

CHAPTER 6

ANBENOWL POTION

Betty had the week off of school. They needed to find a new potion teacher but now everybody knew about school lane. People were going there 4 times a week.

On Monday, Betty went to four shops. She looked at books called 'creatures of all kind', 'all around the Solar system', 'guide of how how to use an umbrella' and 'the future is coming'.

On Tuesday, Betty went to her lessons on 'changing a pot 'and 'everything history'. On Wednesday, Betty went to one lesson on potion mixing and she kept doing that all the way to Saturday. However on Sunday,

Betty crept in to the potions class room and looked for some potions that were not at school lane. There was only one. It was Anbenowl potion.

Anbenowl potion was known to give you luck on the 3rd day of every month. Betty put that potion in her purse just in case she wanted some. Betty waited four days and then it was time to use that potion.

Luckily Betty's new potion teacher was one of the nicest teacher's in Betty's school so Betty decided to put it back in the potions classroom. Betty had already taken a little bit out and drank some because it was good luck that the potion teacher did not notice. In fact the potion teacher nearly thought he had drank it himself and forgotten.

CHAPTER 7

BETTY'S FIFTEENTH BIRTHDAY

It was near Betty's birthday because it was the sixth to last day of school. Betty was having her birthday party early. She decorated her bedroom with signs saying 'HAPPY BIRTHDAY!!!' and made lists saying what she would like to do.

On the gate leading outside she put up a sign saying it is Betty's birthday soon. 'Please come to floor four, number six' the signs read. On her birthday, she received lots of presents and cards. Her favourite card said…

'Dear Betty,

I am very proud of you for fighting the night jogger. Your present will come soon and I will see you the day after tomorrow.

From Krank'

At Betty's school, when it was somebody's birthday, they would let the birthday person have two weeks off. Betty spent one week at school lane and one week at her parents house. When Betty got back, she had a big rest for four weekends.

Luckily in a couple of days, Betty will get her luck. Betty loved her birthday and this one was her second favourite birthday of her whole life. Betty was excited to get that luck and was thinking of what it could be when she went to bed.

CHAPTER 8

THE UNDERPOINT

Betty was walking to school lane to return the books she had borrowed from the school lane library, when suddenly she got sucked in to a secret room. Betty forgot to pull the school lane bar and there was no time to get back up. She accidentally pulled the wrong bar.

"Betty, oh Betty" someone said behind her. Betty turned around and saw Jace, who mercifully rubbed Betty's back and said "Betty are are you ok". Betty replied "yes what are you doing here?". Jace smiled and said "I'm here to see what you are doing here". "Well... I accidentally pulled the wrong bar" Betty said. "Well... since you're here I can give a tour" Jace responded. "um um ok" said Betty.

They walked down a dark corridor, past an old broken mirror, to a four hundred year old arena. Jace said "they still use this arena to this day".

They got to a very stinky room which was filled with rotten bones and followed that corridor of bones until they got to another room. There was a circle on a large door and in the middle it read 'This is the vault of Ezra the odd'. "Ezra the odd?" Jace asked. "Yes" Betty answered. "He made this room. See... there are three stones, each said to be a part of him" said Jace.

They then got to a room with three tall mirrors. Jace pulled out a red stone and held it towards the biggest mirror in the middle. On each side were two smaller mirrors. "This place is called the underpoint." said jace before they both jumped through the big middle mirror. It was like getting sucked into that secret room to get to school lane, the horizon or the underpoint, but it was electric and it didn't hurt.

On the other side, they were back at school lane. Jace took Betty to the horizon before going home.

CHAPTER 9

THE BATTLE FOR THE HORIZON

After Jace had left, a strange man appeared on the horizon. He looked suspicious. Betty saw that man talking to the horizon angels. She wanted to tell Jace but also wanted to confront this man.

"fu fu fu fu fairies" the man whispered. "Yes, fairies" said Betty. "Did you think I would never find you Betty?" said the man. The man plucked a fairy out of the air and squeezed it towards Betty so that it's venom would get on her.

Just then, the horizon angels' venom started pouring like rain does and it was hot where the man was. Betty flung her umbrella. "o ow hu hu hu hu…" the man said, dodging Betty's umbrella. "B.. B.. Betty are you a a…." said the Man. "Am I a what? said Betty. "My name is Krank" the man replied sternly. Finally the angel venom stopped.

Krank ran towards Betty and stole her umbrella before putting his hand on Betty's head. Luckily it was the day that Betty had her luck! Krank tripped over his shoelaces. The wind was blowing heavily but Betty felt lucky and had enough time to get out her umbrella and fight back.

It was a miracle! Betty stopped Krank! Betty banished him from the horizon and teleported back to Mr and Mrs Bark in time for the start of her 10th school year.

❖

Betty's adventure continues in...

Betty and the Surge of School Mysteries

ABOUT THE AUTHOR

Age: 7

Pets: Hamster and goldfish

Favourite Series: Harry Potter, Horrible History, Horrible Science, The Knowledge

Did you know: Every character in Betty is named after someone I know.

Printed in Great Britain
by Amazon

33016431R00020